This Book Belongs To

SHIRLEY TEMPLE'S NURSERY TALES

ILLUSTRATED BY J. P. MILLER

RANDOM HOUSE • NEW YORK

·C·O·N·T·E·N·T·S·

- The Rooster, the Mouse, and the Little Red Hen

- The Old Woman and Her Pig

- The Three Bears

- Jack and the Beanstalk

- Henny Penny

- The Elves and the Shoemaker

- The Tale of Peter Rabbit

- The Pedlar's Pack

The ROOSTER, the MOUSE, and the LITTLE RED HEN

Once upon a time there was a hill, and on the hill there was a pretty little house. It had one little green door and four little windows with green shutters; and in it there lived a rooster and a mouse and a little red hen.

On this particular morning, sad to say, the rooster and the mouse had both gotten out of bed on the wrong side. The rooster said the day was too hot, and the mouse complained because it was too cold. They came grumbling down to the kitchen where the good little red hen, looking as bright as a sunbeam, was bustling about.

"Who'll get some sticks to light the fire?" she asked.

"I shan't," said the rooster.

"I shan't," said the mouse.

"Then I'll do it myself," said the little red hen.

So she ran to get the sticks.

"And now, who'll fill the kettle from the spring?" she asked.

"I shan't," said the rooster.

"I shan't," said the mouse.

"Then I'll do it myself," said the little red hen. And off she ran to fill the kettle.

"And who'll get the breakfast ready?" she asked, as she put the kettle on to boil.

"I shan't," said the rooster.

"I shan't," said the mouse.

"I'll do it myself," said the little red hen.

All through breakfast the rooster and the mouse quarreled and grumbled. The rooster upset the milk jug, and the mouse scattered crumbs upon the floor.

"Who'll clear away the breakfast?" asked the poor little red hen, hoping they would soon leave off being cross.

"I shan't," said the rooster.

"I shan't," said the mouse.

"Then I'll do it myself," said the little red hen.

So she cleared everything away, swept up the crumbs, and brushed the fireplace.

"And now, who'll help me make the beds?"

"I shan't," said the rooster.

"I shan't," said the mouse.

"Then I'll do it myself," said the little red hen. And she tripped away upstairs. But the lazy rooster and mouse each sat down in a comfortable armchair by the fire and soon fell fast asleep.

Now on another hill close by was another little house. It was very ugly. It had a door that wouldn't shut, and two broken windows, and all the paint was off the shutters. In this house there lived a bold bad fox who for some time had had his eye on the rooster and the mouse and the little plump red hen.

On this particular morning, Mr. Fox gathered up his great sack, crept up the hill and sneaked quietly into the garden of his neighbors. If the rooster and the mouse hadn't been asleep, they would have seen his sharp eyes peeping in at the window.

Rat-tat-tat-tat, Rat-tat-tat, the fox knocked at the door.

"Who can that be?" said the mouse, half opening his eyes.

"Go and look for yourself, if you want to know," said the rude rooster.

"It's the postman, perhaps," thought the mouse, "and he may have a letter for me." So without waiting to see who it was, he lifted the latch and opened the door. As

soon as he opened it, in jumped the big fox, with a cruel smile on his face!

"Oh! oh! oh!" squeaked the mouse, as he tried to run up the chimney.

"Doodle-doodle-do!" screamed the rooster, as he jumped on the back of the biggest armchair.

But the fox only laughed; and without more ado he took the little mouse by the tail and popped him into the sack, and seized the rooster by the tail and popped him in too.

When the poor little red hen came running downstairs to see what all the noise was about, the fox caught her and put her into the sack with the others. Then he took a long piece of string out of his pocket, wound it round and round and round the mouth of the sack, and tied it very tight. Throwing the sack over his back, he set off down the hill.

"Oh, I wish I hadn't been so cross!" said the rooster, as they went bumping about in the fox's great sack.

"Oh, I wish I hadn't been so lazy!" said the mouse, wiping his eyes with the tip of his tail.

"It's never too late to mend," said the little red hen. "And don't be too sad. See—here I have my little workbag, and in it there is a pair of scissors, and a little thimble, and a needle and thread. Very soon you will see what I am going to do."

Now the sun was very hot, and before long Mr. Fox began to feel his sack was heavy. At last he thought he would lie down under a tree and go to sleep for a little while. So he threw the sack down with a big bump, and very soon fell fast asleep.

Snore, snore, snore, went the fox.

As soon as the little red hen heard this, she took out her scissors and began to snip a hole in the sack, just large enough for the mouse to creep through.

"Quick!" she whispered to the mouse. "Run as fast as you can and bring back a stone just as large as yourself."

Out scampered the mouse, and soon came back, dragging the stone after him.

"Push it in here," said the little red hen; and in he pushed it in a twinkling.

Then the little red hen snipped away at the hole till it was large enough for the rooster to get through.

"Quick!" she said. "Run now, and get a stone as big as yourself."

Out flew the rooster, and soon came back, quite out of breath, with a big stone which he pushed into the sack too.

Then the little red hen popped out and got a stone as big as herself, and pushed it in. Next she put on her thimble, took out her needle and thread, and sewed up the hole as quickly as ever she could. When it was done, the rooster and the mouse and the little red hen ran home very fast, shut the door after them, drew the bolts, shut the shutters, pulled down the blinds, and felt quite safe.

The fox lay fast asleep under the tree for some time, but at last he woke up.

"Dear, dear!" he said, rubbing his eyes and then looking at the long shadows on the grass. "How late it is getting! I must hurry home."

So the wicked fox went grumbling and groaning down the hill till he came to the stream. Splash! In went one foot. Splash! In went the other. But the stones in the sack were so heavy that, at the very next step, down tumbled Mr. Fox into a deep pool. And that was the last that anybody ever saw of him.

The rooster and the mouse never grumbled again. They lit the fire, filled the kettle, laid the breakfast table, and did all the work, while the good little red hen had a holiday, resting in the big armchair.

No foxes ever troubled them again, and for all I know they are still living happily in the little house with the green door and green shutters, which stands on the hill.

THE OLD WOMAN AND HER PIG

One day an old woman was sweeping her hearth and she found among the ashes a dented coin. "I will go to the village and buy a fat pig with this coin," she said to herself. So she went and bought a pig and began to walk home with it.

But when they came to the end of the village the pig refused to jump over the stile. Seeing a dog by the roadside, the old woman said, "Dog, dog, bite pig. Pig won't jump over the stile and I shan't get home tonight." But the dog would not.

Near by the old woman spied a stick, so she said to the stick, "Stick, stick, beat dog. Dog won't bite pig, pig won't jump over the stile and I shan't get home tonight." But the stick would not.

Some brush was burning not far off, and the old woman called, "Fire, fire, burn stick. Stick won't beat dog, dog won't bite pig, pig won't jump over the stile and I shan't get home tonight." But the fire would not.

On the other side of the road was a deep pool of water, and the old woman cried, "Water, water, quench fire. Fire won't burn stick, stick won't beat dog, dog won't bite pig, pig won't jump over the stile and I shan't get home tonight." But the water would not.

A black ox grazed near by. The old woman shouted to it, saying, "Ox, ox, drink water. Water won't quench fire, fire won't burn stick, stick won't beat dog, dog won't bite pig, pig won't jump over the stile and I shan't get home tonight." But the ox would not.

Now the village butcher was passing by and to him the old woman said, "Butcher, butcher, kill ox. Ox won't drink water, water won't quench fire, fire won't burn stick, stick won't beat dog, dog won't bite pig, pig won't jump over the stile and I shan't get home tonight." But the butcher would not.

To a rope hanging over the fence the old woman cried, "Rope, rope, hang butcher. Butcher won't kill ox, ox won't drink water, water won't quench fire, fire won't burn stick, stick won't beat dog, dog won't bite pig, pig won't jump over the stile and I shan't get home tonight." But the rope would not.

A rat ran along the fence rail and the old woman called to it, "Rat, rat, gnaw rope. Rope won't hang butcher, butcher won't kill ox, ox won't drink water, water won't quench fire, fire won't burn stick, stick won't beat dog, dog won't bite pig, pig won't jump over the stile and I shan't get home tonight." But the rat would not.

"Cat," said the cow, "if yonder farmer will give me some clover, I will give you a bowl of milk."

Now the old woman's fortunes changed! The farmer gave the cow some clover, the cow gave the cat a bowl of milk, the cat began to catch the rat, the rat began to gnaw the rope, the rope began to hang the butcher, the butcher began to kill the ox, the ox began to drink the water, the water began to quench the fire, the fire began to burn the stick, the stick began to beat the dog, the dog began to bite the pig, the pig at last jumped over the stile, and the old woman did get home that night.

A farm cat came along the road and to it the old woman said in a quavery voice, "Cat, cat, catch rat. Rat won't gnaw rope, rope won't hang butcher, butcher won't kill ox, ox won't drink water, water won't quench fire, fire won't burn stick, stick won't beat dog, dog won't bite pig, pig won't jump over the stile and I shan't get home tonight."

The cat thought a moment, then she said, "If yonder cow will give me a bowl of milk I will do as you say." And she asked the cow for some milk.

THE THREE BEARS

In a sunny clearing in a dark woods there once lived three bears: a great, huge father bear, a middle-sized mother bear, and a wee, small baby bear. They were gentle bears and kept their little house neat as a pin.

One morning when Mother Bear had prepared the breakfast porridge and poured it into three bowls, she put on her bonnet and said, "Come, we'll go for a walk in the woods while our breakfast porridge cools. It is

now too hot to eat." So they all set out—the great, huge father bear, the middle-sized mother bear, and the wee, small baby bear.

Now it chanced that a little girl named Goldilocks, playing in the woods, saw the bears' little house. She went up to it and knocked at the door. There was no answer, and, being a very curious little girl, she peeped through the keyhole. She saw no one, so she opened

the door and went inside. She was tired now, so she sat down in the great, huge father bear's chair, but it was too hard. She tried the middle-sized mother bear's chair, but it was too soft. Then she sat in the wee, small baby bear's chair and found it just right. But alas, she was too heavy for it and broke through its seat of rushes!

By this time Goldilocks was hungry so she went to the kitchen, and there on the table she spied the three bowls of porridge. She tasted the porridge in the great, huge bowl but it was too hot. She tasted from the middle-sized bowl but that was too cold. At last she tried the porridge in the wee, small bowl and that was just right. So she ate it all up!

Soon Goldilocks began to feel sleepy, so she went upstairs to the bedroom. Here were three beds, neatly made. She scrambled up on the great, huge bed but it was too high at the head for her. Then she tried the middle-sized bed but it was much too low at the foot for her. At last she crept into the wee, small bed and it was just right. So she fell asleep!

Now the bears returned from their walk in the woods.

The great, huge father bear looked at his chair, and said in his big deep voice, "Somebody's been sitting in my chair!"

The middle-sized mother bear looked at hers and said in her middle-sized voice, "Somebody's been sitting in my chair, too!"

And the wee, small baby bear cried in his wee, small voice, "Somebody's been sitting in my chair and has broken it all to pieces!"

In the kitchen, Father Bear uncovered his great, huge porridge bowl. "Well," he said in his big deep

voice, "somebody's been tasting my porridge!"

Then Mother Bear uncovered her middle-sized bowl and said in her middle-sized voice, "Somebody's been tasting my porridge, too!"

The wee, small baby bear took one look at his empty bowl and began to cry. "Somebody's been tasting my porridge and has eaten it all up!"

Soon the three bears went upstairs. "Tut, tut," said the great, huge father bear. "Somebody's certainly been sleeping in my bed!"

"And, indeed, somebody's been sleeping in my bed, too!" said the middle-sized mother bear.

"Look!" cried the wee, small baby bear. "Somebody's been in my bed—and here she is!"

Goldilocks was awakened by the wee, small baby bear's piping voice. She opened her eyes and saw the three bears looking down at her, three friendly bears who meant her no harm. But Goldilocks did not know they were friendly. She leaped from the wee, small baby bear's bed and ran to the window. Out she jumped and ran away home as fast as she could.

As for the three bears, they never saw her again, and for all I know, they still live happily in the sunny clearing deep in the dark woods.

Jack and the Beanstalk

O nce upon a time there was a boy named Jack who lived with his mother in a bare little house. They were very poor, for Jack's father was dead. And all the boy and his mother had to live on was the milk their cow gave them every morning.

But one morning the cow stopped giving milk, and then there was nothing at all to eat.

"What shall we do now?" asked Jack, who was a good boy at heart.

"You will have to take the cow to market and sell her," his mother answered. "Then we will be able to buy some food."

So Jack tied a rope around the cow's neck and led her down the dusty road toward town.

He hadn't gone far when he met a funny-looking old man who said to him, "Good morning, Jack."

"Good morning to you," said Jack, wondering how the old man knew his name.

"And where are you off to?" asked the man.

"I'm going to market to sell our cow."

"What will you take for her?" the old man asked.

"Anything I can get," Jack answered.

"Let *me* have her," said the old man, "and I will give you this handful of magic beans."

"Magic beans!" cried Jack.

"Yes, indeed. Plant them before you go to bed and by morning you'll have a bean vine as high as the sky."

"You don't say," said Jack. And he gave the old man his cow, took the colored beans in exchange, and hurried home.

When Jack's mother saw the beans she burst into tears and tossed them out the window. "How could you be so foolish?" she exclaimed. And without giving the boy a chance to tell her they were magic beans, she cuffed him and sent him straight to bed.

In the morning when Jack started to get out of bed, he noticed that the room shone with a strange green light. Enormous green leaves covered his windowpane.

Dashing into his clothes, Jack rushed out of doors. And what do you think he saw? A giant beanstalk that grew straight up into the sky.

"It must have grown from my beans," Jack said, staring upward. "They were magic beans after all."

Grasping the stalk firmly with his hands and knees, Jack started climbing. He climbed and he climbed and he climbed till at last he was up among the clouds. And there in front of him stood a castle—a gray stone castle with tall pointed turrets.

Walking boldly over to the doorstep, he knocked at the big wooden door. His long climb had made him hungry and he thought he would ask for something to eat.

After a considerable wait, the door creaked slowly open and a great towering woman peered out at Jack with fear and amazement.

"Oh, please mum, do give me a bite," said Jack. "I've had nothing to eat since yesterday morning."

"Go away! Go away!" the woman cried in terror. "My husband is a giant. If he comes home and finds you here, he will surely eat you."

But Jack was so hungry and pleaded so hard that finally the giant's wife took pity on him. "Well, come along then," she said. "I'll give you some bread and a bowl of porridge. But mind you hurry!"

Jack had barely sat down by the kitchen stove when he heard a loud thump, thump, thump on the stairs. The floor shook and the walls trembled.

"Quick! My husband is coming," the woman whispered. "Hide in here," and she pushed Jack inside the oven.

Thump, thump, thump. The steps came closer, and into the room stomped a huge man, twice the size of the woman and frightful to behold.

"Fee, fi, fo, fum," he roared, "I smell the blood of an

Englishman."

"Nonsense, dear," said the giant's wife. "It's your breakfast you smell." And when the giant saw the roast of mutton on the table, he fell to at once and started carving.

At last he finished stuffing himself. "Wife!" he shouted. "Bring me my gold!"

The woman quickly took two heavy money bags out of an enormous chest and laid them on the table. Whereupon the giant played with his gold pieces until at last he dozed off in his chair, snoring so hard that the dishes rattled in the closet.

Then Jack crept quietly out of the oven and up onto the table. Taking one of the bags under his arm, he slid back down to the floor and ran for his life. The giant was sleeping so hard he never woke up.

When Jack's mother saw the gold pieces she wept for joy.

"You see, Mother, I was right," Jack told her. "Those were magic beans."

As it happened, there were enough gold coins in the bag to keep Jack and his mother in comfort for a whole year. But at the end of that time the last coin had been spent and Jack decided to climb the beanstalk again.

Once more the kindly giant's wife took pity on him and invited him in for a bite to eat. And once more the giant came roaring in, this time while Jack was finishing his piece of cake.

The woman hustled the boy off into a woodbox she kept behind her stove.

"Fee, fi, fo, fum," roared the giant, "I smell the blood of an Englishman."

But his wife coaxed him into thinking he smelled the sizzling ox that was turning on the spit. And when she brought the heaping platter to the table he fell to with a smack and a roar, eating until he had licked the platter bare.

When he was finished, the giant leaned back and stretched. "Wife, bring me my magic hen," he cried. "Bring the hen that lays the golden eggs."

The woman immediately set a small speckled hen on the table before him.

"Lay!" commanded the giant, and the hen laid a shining gold egg. "Lay another," he cried, and the hen laid another—and another and another as the giant continued to give the command.

Jack, peeking out of the woodbox, had never seen anything half so wonderful.

Finally, when there were golden eggs heaped all over the table, the giant fell asleep again. The rumble of his snores rattled the pots and pans and shook the window panes.

Quickly Jack climbed out of the woodbox, picked up the hen, and went sliding down the beanstalk again. His mother watched with amazement while he ordered the speckled hen to lay her golden eggs on their kitchen table.

Now Jack should have been satisfied with his magic hen, for the golden eggs brought him all the money he could possibly need. But still he kept on thinking of the giant's castle, until finally one day he decided to climb the beanstalk once again.

This time he knew better than to go straight to the giant's castle. Instead he crept behind a bush until he saw the giant's wife come out with a pail of water. Then he ran into the kitchen and hid inside the copper kettle.

He hadn't been there long when he heard a thump! thump! thump! And in came the giant roaring,

"Fee, fie, fo, fum,
I smell the blood of an Englishman
But be he live, or be he dead,
I'll grind his bones to make me bread."

And this time the giant searched all over the kitchen to see what he could find. He looked inside the oven. He raised the lid and peered into the woodbox. But fortunately he never thought of looking inside the copper kettle.

While he ate he kept muttering, "I would have sworn I smelled——"

When at last he had finished his meal, the giant sat back.

"Now bring me my golden harp," he shouted. And his wife brought a small golden harp and placed it on the table.

The giant looked at the harp. "Play!" he commanded. And the harp played such soft, sweet music that soon both the giant and his wife fell asleep.

When Jack heard the giant's snores he lifted the kettle lid very quietly and got down like a mouse, creeping on hands and knees till he came to the table. There he raised himself up ever so softly and seized the magic harp.

But no sooner had he touched the harp than it called out, "Master! Master! Awake!"

The giant jumped up and ran with big strides after Jack. But Jack was already halfway down the beanstalk before the giant lowered himself onto the thick stem. The vine swayed and shook under the giant's weight.

As Jack's nimble feet touched ground, he cried:

"Mother! Mother! Bring me the hatchet! Quick!"

His mother came running. Jack grabbed the hatchet and chopped the beanstalk in two with a mighty blow. Down crashed the giant with a terrible thump, and to this day there is a deep hole where he sank out of sight into the ground.

Jack's mother was so pleased to see her dear son home safe and sound that she cooked him a fine meal almost big enough for a giant to eat. Then Jack showed his mother the golden harp, and what with showing that and selling the golden eggs, Jack and his mother became quite rich and lived happily ever after, though Jack was careful never again to plant any beans that looked the least bit strange.

HENNY PENNY

One morning an acorn fell, *plop,* on the head of Henny Penny as she scratched for beetles in the garden. "Mercy," said she, "the sky is falling! I must hurry and tell the king."

So Henny Penny hurried off. She had not gone far when she met handsome Cocky Locky. "Oh, do come along," Henny Penny urged. "The sky is falling! We must hurry and tell the king."

So they went along and they went along and after only a short walk they met Drakey Lakey. "Come along, come along," called Cocky Locky. "The sky is falling! We must hurry and tell the king."

So Drakey Lakey joined Henny Penny and Cocky Locky. And they went along and they went along until they met Goosey Loosey. "Come along, *do* come along," cried Drakey Lakey. "The sky is falling! We must hurry and tell the king."

Goosey Loosey fell into step beside Henny Penny, Cocky Locky and Drakey Lakey. And they went along and they went along until they saw Turkey Lurkey coming down the road. "Come along, come along," cried Goosey Loosey. "The sky is falling! We must hurry and tell the king."

So Turkey Lurkey joined Henny Penny, Cocky Locky, Drakey Lakey and Goosey Loosey. And they went along and they went along until, at a turn in the road, they saw Foxy Loxy slipping through the grass. "Come along, come along," gobbled Turkey Lurkey. "The sky is falling! We must hurry and tell the king."

"Ah, come with me instead," answered Foxy Loxy. "I will show you a shortcut to the king's palace . . . but only one of you at a time. You come first." He motioned to Turkey Lurkey.

Foolish Turkey Lurkey followed Foxy Loxy down a passage where his hungry family waited. Once inside the den, *whrumph!* Off came Turkey Lurkey's head and into the pot he went.

"Now you next," called Foxy Loxy to Goosey Loosey. And into the pot she went. Then Drakey Lakey and Cocky Locky followed until only Henny Penny remained.

But when Cocky Locky saw how they had him tricked, he let out one loud crow before Foxy Loxy could stop him.

"Why, Cocky Locky is crowing. It must be morning," said Henny Penny to herself. And she ruffled her feathers. "High time for me to go home and lay my morning egg."

So Henny Penny forgot to tell the king the sky was falling. Instead, she hurried home to lay her morning egg, a much more sensible thing to do.

THE ELVES AND THE SHOEMAKER

There was once an old shoemaker who, through no fault of his own, had become so poor he had only enough leather for one pair of shoes.

"Look, wife," he said. "I'll cut these out this evening before we go to bed. Then in the morning I can finish them."

After the job was done he said his prayers, lay down, and fell asleep.

In the morning, when he went back to his work, the shoemaker discovered a pair of shoes standing finished on his workbench.

"What can this mean?" he said in astonishment. He examined the shoes carefully and found that not a stitch was out of place. They were as good as the work of the very best shoemakers. The poor old shoemaker could not understand this strange happening in the least.

Soon a customer came in. "What fine shoes!" he exclaimed. And he was so pleased he offered a great deal of money for them—enough so that the shoemaker was able to buy leather for two more pairs.

That evening the old man cut out the leather and left the pieces on the workbench as before. In the morning, to his surprise, he discovered two more pairs of shoes standing, already finished, on the workbench. Like the others, these shoes were sewn with the greatest care.

"What well-made shoes!" the customers exclaimed when they entered his shop. And they paid so well for the shoes that the old shoemaker was able to buy leather for four more pairs. Again he cut out the shoes in the evening, and again he found them all beautifully made when he went into his shop in the morning.

And so it went. Each night, before going to bed, the shoemaker would cut out his leather; and every morning when he went into his shop he would find the pieces all made up into the neatest shoes imaginable. Before long he was making so much money he was well on his way to becoming rich.

Now it happened that one evening, not long before Christmas, the shoemaker said to his wife, "How would it be if we sat up all night and watched to see who is helping us?"

"That's a fine idea," said his wife. So they lit a

candle and hid behind some coats that were hanging in a corner of the shop. Then they waited and watched.

On the stroke of midnight came two little elves who sat down at the shoemaker's workbench and set busily to work. They took up the pieces of leather and began stitching and hammering so quickly with their nimble little fingers that the shoemaker and his wife could hardly believe their eyes. The tiny men never stopped until everything was finished and all the shoes stood ready on the workbench. Then they skipped lightly out of the room, closing the door quietly behind them.

Next morning the good wife said to her husband, "Those dear little elves have brought us such good luck, wouldn't it be nice if we could do something for them? They must be very cold, running about with so few clothes. Why don't I make them some warm little coats and socks, and you can make them some tiny shoes."

The shoemaker thought this an excellent plan. While his wife stitched and knitted, he worked busily at making the tiniest little leather shoes you have ever seen.

At last everything was ready. On the night before Christmas, the old couple laid their presents on the workbench and then hid in the corner to see what the little men would do.

At midnight the elves came skipping in, ready to set to work as usual. But instead of the pieces of leather already cut out, they found the pretty little clothes the shoemaker and his wife had laid out for them. At first they were amazed, then delighted. Quickly they slipped into their new clothes and skipped around, singing:

"Tonight we have no need to sew——
We'll wear these clothes and off we'll go!"

Then they hopped and danced about some more, jumping over the stools and tables until at last they ran out the door. From that time they were never seen again, but all went well with the old shoemaker and his wife as long as they lived and the old man had good luck in everything he did.

THE TALE of PETER RABBIT

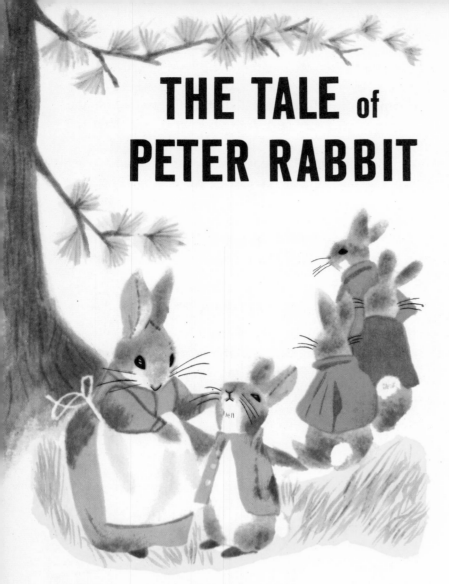

<big>O</big>nce upon a time there were four little rabbits, and their names were—
> Flopsy,
> Mopsy,
> Cotton-tail,
> and Peter.

They lived with their mother in a sandbank, underneath the root of a very big fir tree.

"Now, my dears," said old Mrs. Rabbit one morning, "you may go into the fields or down the lane, but don't go into Mr. McGregor's garden: your father had an accident there; he was put in a pie by Mrs. McGregor.

"Now run along, and don't get into mischief. I am going out."

Then old Mrs. Rabbit took a basket and her umbrella, and went through the wood to the baker's. She bought a loaf of brown bread and five currant buns.

Flopsy, Mopsy and Cotton-tail, who were good little bunnies, went down the lane to gather blackberries.

But Peter, who was very naughty, ran straight away to Mr. McGregor's garden, and squeezed under the gate!

First he ate some lettuces and some French beans; and then he ate some radishes.

And then, feeling rather sick, he went to look for some parsley.

But round the end of a cucumber frame, whom should he meet but Mr. McGregor!

Mr. McGregor was on his hands and knees planting out young cabbages, but he jumped up and ran after Peter, waving a rake and calling out, "Stop thief!"

Peter was most dreadfully frightened; he rushed all over the garden, for he had forgotten the way back to the gate.

He lost one of his shoes among the cabbages, and the other shoe amongst the potatoes.

After losing them, he ran on four legs and went faster, so that I think he might have got away altogether if he had not unfortunately run into a gooseberry net, and got caught by the large buttons on his jacket. It was a blue jacket with brass buttons, quite new.

Peter gave himself up for lost, and shed big tears; but his sobs were overheard by some friendly sparrows, who flew to him in great excitement, and implored him to exert himself.

Mr. McGregor came up with a sieve, which he intended to pop upon the top of Peter; but Peter wriggled out just in time, leaving his jacket behind him.

And he rushed into the tool shed, and jumped into

a can. It would have been a beautiful thing to hide in, if it had not had so much water in it.

Mr. McGregor was quite sure that Peter was somewhere in the tool shed, perhaps hidden underneath a flowerpot. He began to turn them over carefully, looking under each.

Presently Peter sneezed—"Kertyschoo!" Mr. McGregor was after him in no time, and tried to put his foot upon Peter, who jumped out of a window, upsetting three plants. The window was too small for Mr. McGregor, and he was tired of running after Peter. He went back to his work.

Peter sat down to rest; he was out of breath and trembling with fright, and he had not the least idea which way to go. Also he was very damp from sitting in that can.

After a time he began to wander about, going lippity—lippity—not very fast, and looking all around.

He found a door in a wall; but it was locked, and there was no room for a fat little rabbit to squeeze underneath.

An old mouse was running in and out over the stone doorstep, carrying peas and beans to her family in the wood. Peter asked her the way to the gate, but she had such a large pea in her mouth that she could not answer. She only shook her head at him. Peter began to cry.

Then he tried to find his way straight across the garden, but he became more and more puzzled. Presently, he came to a pond where Mr. McGregor filled his water-cans. A white cat was staring at some goldfish; she sat very, very still, but now and then the tip of her tail twitched as if it were alive. Peter thought it best to go away without speaking to her; he had heard about cats from his cousin, little Benjamin Bunny.

He went back towards the tool shed, but suddenly, quite close to him, he heard the noise of a hoe—scr-r-ritch, scratch, scratch, scritch. Peter scuttered underneath the bushes. But presently, as nothing happened, he came out and climbed upon a wheelbarrow, and peeped over. The first thing he saw was Mr. McGregor hoeing onions. His back was turned towards Peter, and beyond him was the gate!

Peter got down very quietly off the wheelbarrow, and started running as fast as he could go, along a straight walk behind some black-currant bushes.

Mr. McGregor caught sight of him at the corner, but Peter did not care. He slipped underneath the gate, and was safe at last in the woods outside the garden.

Mr. McGregor hung up the little jacket and shoes for a scarecrow to frighten the blackbirds.

Peter never stopped running or looked behind him till he got home to the big fir tree.

He was so tired that he flopped down upon the nice soft sand on the floor of the rabbit hole, and shut his eyes. His mother was busy cooking; she wondered what he had done with his clothes. It was the second little jacket and pair of shoes that Peter had lost in a fortnight!

I am sorry to say that Peter was not very well during the evening.

His mother put him to bed, and made some camomile tea; and she gave a dose of it to Peter!

"One tablespoonful to be taken at bedtime."

But Flopsy, Mopsy, and Cotton-tail had bread and milk and blackberries for supper.

THE PEDLAR'S PACK

A pedlar was toiling along a dusty road, carrying his pack on his back, when he saw a donkey grazing by the wayside. "Good day, friend," said he. "If you have nothing to do, perhaps you would not mind carrying my load for me."

"If I say yes, what will you give me?" asked the donkey.

"I will give you two pieces of gold," said the pedlar. But he did not speak the truth, for he knew he had no gold to give.

"Agreed," said the donkey. So they journeyed on together in a very friendly manner, the donkey carrying the pedlar's pack, and the pedlar walking by his side. After a time they met a raven, who was looking for worms in the roadside.

"Good day, friend," the donkey called out. "If you are going our way you might as well sit on my back and drive away the flies."

"And what will you pay me for doing this?" asked the raven.

"Money is no object to me," bragged the donkey. "I will give you three pieces of gold." And he too knew he was making a false promise, for he had no gold at all.

"Agreed," said the raven. So they went on in high good humor, the donkey carrying the pedlar's pack, and the raven sitting on the donkey's back driving away the flies.

After a time they met a sparrow. The raven called out, "Good day, little cousin. If you want to earn a little money, bring me some worms from the bank as we go along. I am very hungry, for I had no breakfast."

"What will you give me if I do?" asked the sparrow.

"Four pieces of gold," said the raven grandly. "I have saved more during my long life than I know how to spend." Of course he knew this was not true, for he had not saved any gold at all.

"Very well," said the sparrow, and on they went—the donkey carrying the pedlar's pack, the raven keeping the flies away from the donkey, and the sparrow bringing worms to the raven.

Presently they saw a good-sized town in the distance. The pedlar took some shawls from his pack and hung them over the donkey's back for the townspeople to see and buy. On top of the shawls he placed a small scarlet blanket.

When the sparrow saw the blanket he said to the pedlar, "What will you take for that little blanket? It seems a good one. Name your price and you shall have whatever it is, for I am badly in need of a blanket just now." But as it happened, the sparrow hadn't a penny in the world and knew he couldn't pay for it.

"The price of the blanket is five pieces of gold," said the pedlar.

"That seems a little costly to me," said the sparrow. "I will give you four pieces of gold but not five."

"Agreed," said the pedlar. And he chuckled to himself, thinking, "Now I shall be able to pay the donkey. Otherwise I might have had trouble in getting rid of him."

The sparrow flew to the raven's side and whispered in his ear, "Will you please pay me the four pieces of gold you owe me? We are coming to a town now, and I must be turning back."

"Four pieces of gold is really too much for bringing a few worms," said the raven. "But I will be glad to give you three at once." And the raven bent down over the donkey's ear and whispered:

"My friend, it is time you paid the three pieces of gold you promised me for keeping the flies off your back."

"On thinking it over," said the donkey, "I have decided that three pieces of gold are really a great deal too much to give for having a few flies driven away. You must have known I was only joking when I said it. But I will let you have two." And the donkey turned to the pedlar, saying, "Now, good sir, your two pieces of gold, if you please."

"In a moment," answered the pedlar. And he turned to the sparrow, saying, "I really must have the money for the blanket at once."

"So you shall," said the sparrow, and he cried angrily to the raven, "I want my money now. I cannot wait any longer."

"In an instant," answered the raven. And again he whispered to the donkey, "Why can't you pay me honestly? You should be ashamed of trying to slip out of your debts in such a way."

"I won't keep you waiting a second," said the donkey. And he turned once more to the pedlar, crying, "Come, give me my money. For shame! A man like you trying to cheat a poor beast like me."

Then the pedlar said to the sparrow, "Pay me for my blanket, or I'll wring your neck."

And the sparrow cried to the raven, "Give me my money or I'll peck out your eyes."

And the raven croaked to the donkey, "If you don't pay me, I'll bite off your tail."

And the donkey again cried to the pedlar, "You dishonest wretch, pay me my money or I'll kick you soundly!"

They made such an uproar outside the walls of the town that a constable came out to see what it was all about. Each turned to him and began to complain loudly of the other.

"You are a noisy set of troublemakers," said the constable. "I'm going to take you to the mayor and he'll put a quick end to your quarreling." And the constable led them straight to the marketplace, where the mayor sat judging cases.

"Now what have we here?" asked the mayor. "A pedlar, a donkey, a raven and a sparrow. A set of worthless nuisances, I'll be bound! What do you have to say for yourselves?"

At this the pedlar began to complain of the sparrow, and the sparrow of the raven, and the raven of the donkey, and the donkey of the pedlar.

The mayor, meanwhile, was paying little attention to them, for he was busy eyeing the pedlar's pack. Finally he said, "It strikes me that you are a set of good-for-nothing fellows—one quite as bad as the other. I order that the pedlar be locked up in the prison, that the donkey be soundly thrashed, and that the raven and sparrow both have their tail feathers plucked and then be turned out of town. As for the blanket, it seems to me to be at the bottom of all the trouble. Since I cannot allow you to keep the cause of such a disturbance, I will take it for myself. Constable, lead the prisoners away."

The constable did as he was told, and the pedlar was locked up for many days in the prison. "It is very sad to think of what can happen to an honest man," sighed the pedlar. "In the future I shall keep clear of sparrows. If that sparrow had paid me as he ought I wouldn't be here now."

Meantime the donkey was being soundly thrashed, and after each blow he cried, "Alas! alas! See what happens to a poor donkey when he tries to help a human being. If the pedlar had given me the money he owed, I wouldn't be getting this beating. I'll never make another bargain with any man."

The raven and the sparrow hopped out of town by different roads, both feeling very sad about the tail feathers they had lost.

"Alas!" croaked the raven, "my fate is a hard one.

But it serves me right for trusting a donkey who clomps about on his feet and cannot fly. Never again will I trust anything without wings."

The sparrow was so sad he could scarcely hold back his tears. "It all comes from my being so taken in by that raven," he sighed. "But I should have known that so large a bird would never be honest. In the future I will never make a bargain with anything bigger than myself."

But, in truth, they were four of a kind and well deserved exactly what they got.